Ten Little Bunnies

Story by Lisa Bassett
Pictures by Jeni Bassett

JellyBean Press
New York • Avenel, New Jersey

Story Link®
Program

To Mr. and Mrs. Robertson and their grandchildren,
Kenneth and Sarah.

This 1993 edition is published by JellyBean Press, a division of dilithium Press, Ltd.,
distributed by Outlet Book Company, Inc., a Random House Company,
40 Engelhard Avenue, Avenel, New Jersey 07001.

DILITHIUM is a registered trademark and
JELLYBEAN PRESS is a trademark of dilithium Press, Ltd.

Printed and bound in the United States of America

Book design: Melissa Ring • *Cover design: Bill Akunevicz, Jr.*
Production supervision: Roméo Enriquez • *Editorial supervision: Claire Booss*

Library of Congress Cataloging-in-Publication Data
Bassett, Lisa.
Ten little bunnies / story by Lisa Bassett ; pictures by Jeni Bassett.
p. cm.
Summary: After using the Easter Bunny's paints to disguise
themselves, ten mischievous little bunnies are discovered, one by one,
hiding in Mr. Rabbit's garden.
ISBN 0-517-08154-7
[1. Rabbits—Fiction. 2. Gardens—Fiction. 3. Counting.]
I. Bassett, Jeni, ill. II. Title.
PZ7.B2933Te 1993
[E]—dc20   92-37986
                                                         CIP
                                                         AC

8 7 6 5 4 3

One day, Basil Bunny and his nine brothers and sisters were hopping by their father's garden. They all crowded up to the fence and gazed at the rows and rows of leafy vegetables.

"Oh, look at those juicy carrot tops," exclaimed Rosemary.

"And the lettuce! Do you see those big leaves?" cried Pepper.

"I wish we could go into the garden," said Ginger wistfully. "I wish we could taste those cabbages."

"You *know* we are not allowed," said Rosemary.

Basil had been licking his lips and twitching his little whiskers. "What if we could get in without being seen?" he said suddenly. "What if we were nearly invisible?"

"How?" cried all of the little bunnies at once.

"Come on! I have an idea," exclaimed Basil.

The little bunnies followed Basil down the path to the Easter Bunny's house. The Easter Bunny had gone to get eggs from Mrs. Featherwhite, and the windows in his house were dark. The little bunnies pressed their noses to the glass and peered inside.

"I see just what we need!" said Basil, pointing to a high shelf.

The little bunnies crept through the door and helped
Basil get a large jar of paint from the shelf. The label on
the jar said EASTER EGG PAINT. At the bottom of the
label were the words CABBAGE GREEN.

"The Easter Bunny won't mind if we use a little of his green paint," said Basil. He gave a paint brush to each bunny. "Now cover all of your white fur," warned Basil. "If we are cabbage green bunnies, no one will see us in the garden."

As soon as they were coated with green from nose to toe, the bunnies rushed out the door and pattered down the path. They were so eager to get to their father's garden that they never noticed the mess they had left behind.

When they got to the garden they could see their father planting, but he never saw the ten cabbage green bunnies slip under the fence and tiptoe down the rows.

Just as they were about to taste the vegetables, the ten little bunnies heard a familiar voice shouting from down the path.

"Mr. Rabbit! Mr. Rabbit!" called the Easter Bunny. "Somebody took all my green paint! All of it! I can't paint my eggs without green! Mr. Rabbit! My house is covered with green footprints, and look! The footprints lead right to your garden!" The Easter Bunny was hopping up and down, waving the empty jar of cabbage green paint.

Mr. Rabbit hurried to the edge of the garden. "I haven't seen a thief. I haven't seen anyone!" he said.

"Look at these footprints!" cried the Easter Bunny.

"Oh my! Those footprints are small," said Mr. Rabbit, "and there are so many of them. Those footprints look...look like they belong to little bunnies!" Mr. Rabbit and the Easter Bunny looked at each other, and then they looked at the garden.

"I see one!" cried the Easter Bunny, and he dashed
into the garden and snatched a little bunny from under
the tomatoes. Then they found one bunny in the lettuce
leaves.

One on the wheelbarrow.

One among the beans.

One behind the watering can.

One between the cabbages.

One inside a flower pot.

One under the carrot tops.

One beside the hoe.

One among the parsley.

One, two, three, four, five, six, seven, eight, nine, ten
little bunnies bowed their heads until their ears flopped
over their eyes.

"You have been very bad bunnies," said Mr. Rabbit.

"Oh, we are sorry," sniffled all the bunnies at once.
"You have used every drop of my green paint," cried
the Easter Bunny.

"March yourselves right over to Mr. Easter Bunny's house and clean up the mess. Right now!, said Mr. Rabbit sternly.

When the little bunnies got to the Easter Bunny's house, he gave them brushes and buckets of soapy water. Then the Easter Bunny sat glumly in his big armchair, staring at the floor.

"No green," he muttered. "I can't paint my eggs without green." The little bunnies felt miserable.

"Oh, what can we do? How can we ever make this right?" said Basil. The little bunnies shook their heads. "All we can do is clean up this mess. That is all."

They scrubbed as hard as they could. Basil cleaned around the jars of paint, but he scrubbed so hard that he knocked over a jar of yellow.

In his rush to catch the yellow, he knocked over the blue. Suddenly he slipped and skidded into the yellow and blue paint.

The Easter Bunny ran to see what was happening. "Now what?" he cried. "You are making a bigger mess!" But everyone looked at the puddle of paint. The yellow and blue had run together.

"Look! I've made green!" cried Basil. "Mr. Easter Bunny, we can *make* green paint."

The Easter Bunny chewed on his whiskers. "Well, it looks like we *can* make green.

The little bunnies helped the Easter Bunny mix yellow and blue paint to make a big jar of green paint.

The Easter Bunny put the jar of green paint on a shelf and looked at the little bunnies. "You won't be painting yourselves with this green, will you?"

"Never!" cried the little bunnies. The Easter Bunny smiled a smile that meant all the bunnies were forgiven.

That night Mrs. Rabbit gave the little bunnies hot baths with lots of soap.

When they were fluffy and dry, they wiggled their noses happily at the mirror. They saw ten white little bunnies and not a speck of the cabbage green paint.